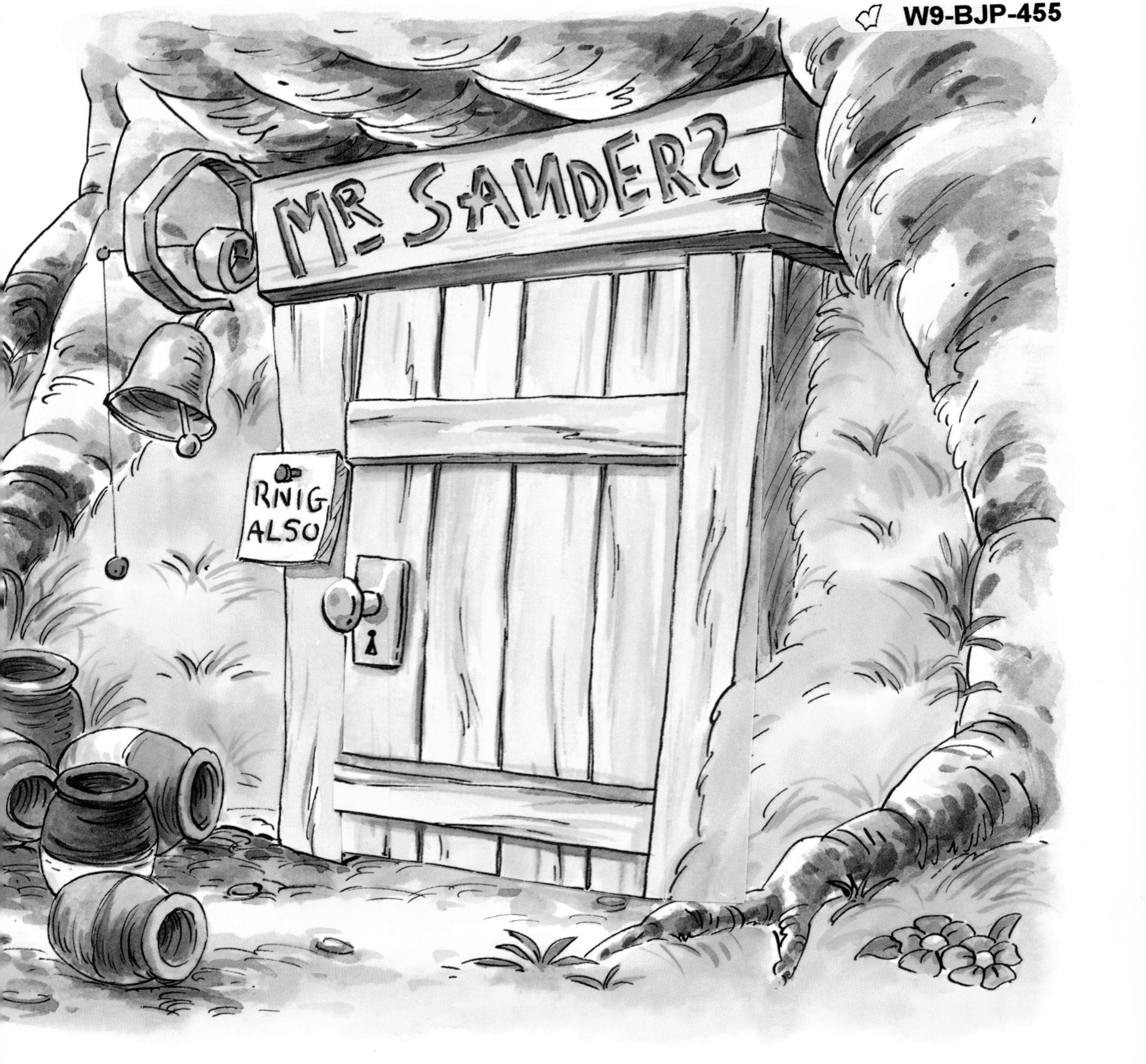

MR SANDERZ
RNIG ALSO

Where is Pooh?
Is he under the bush?

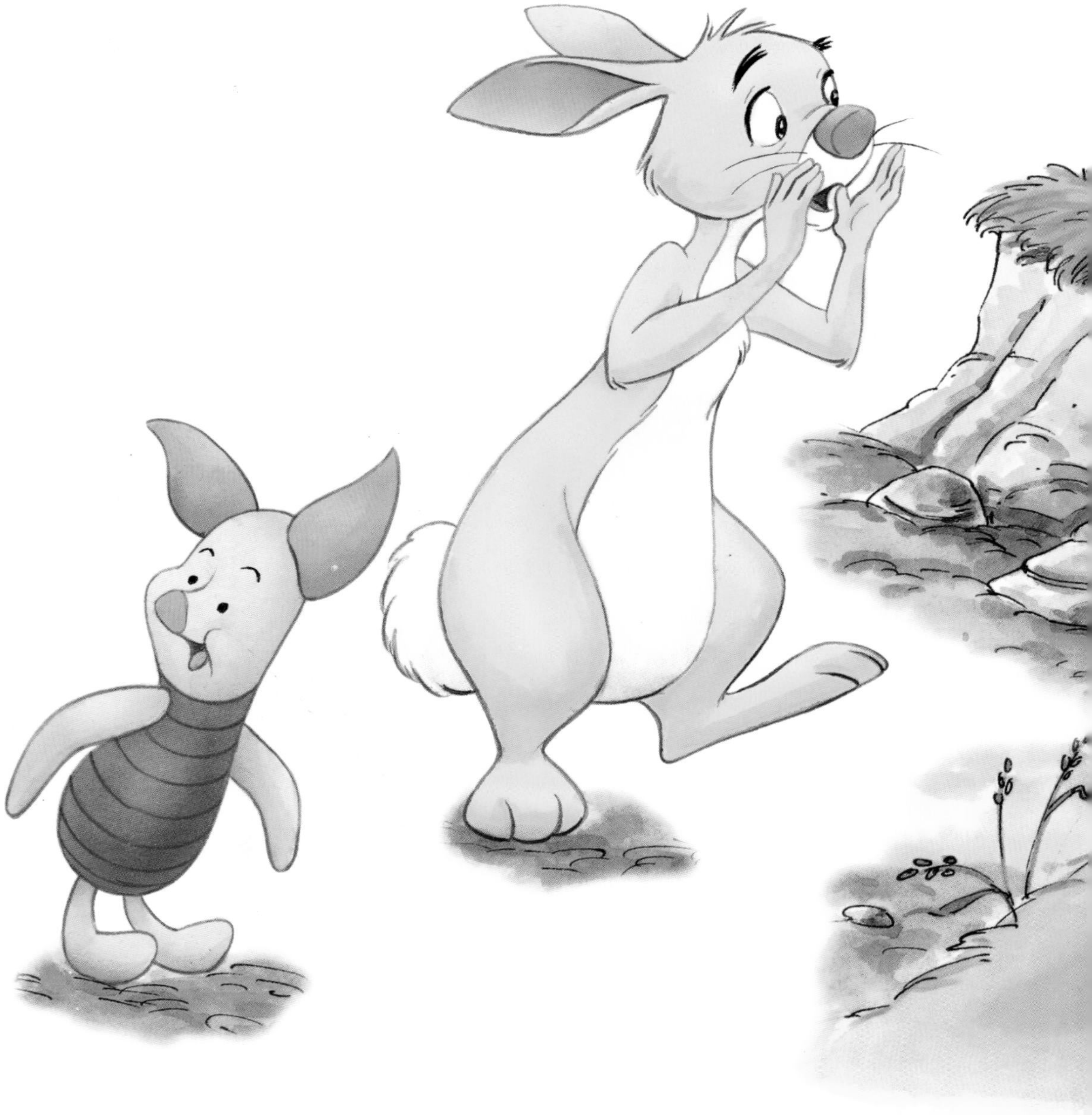

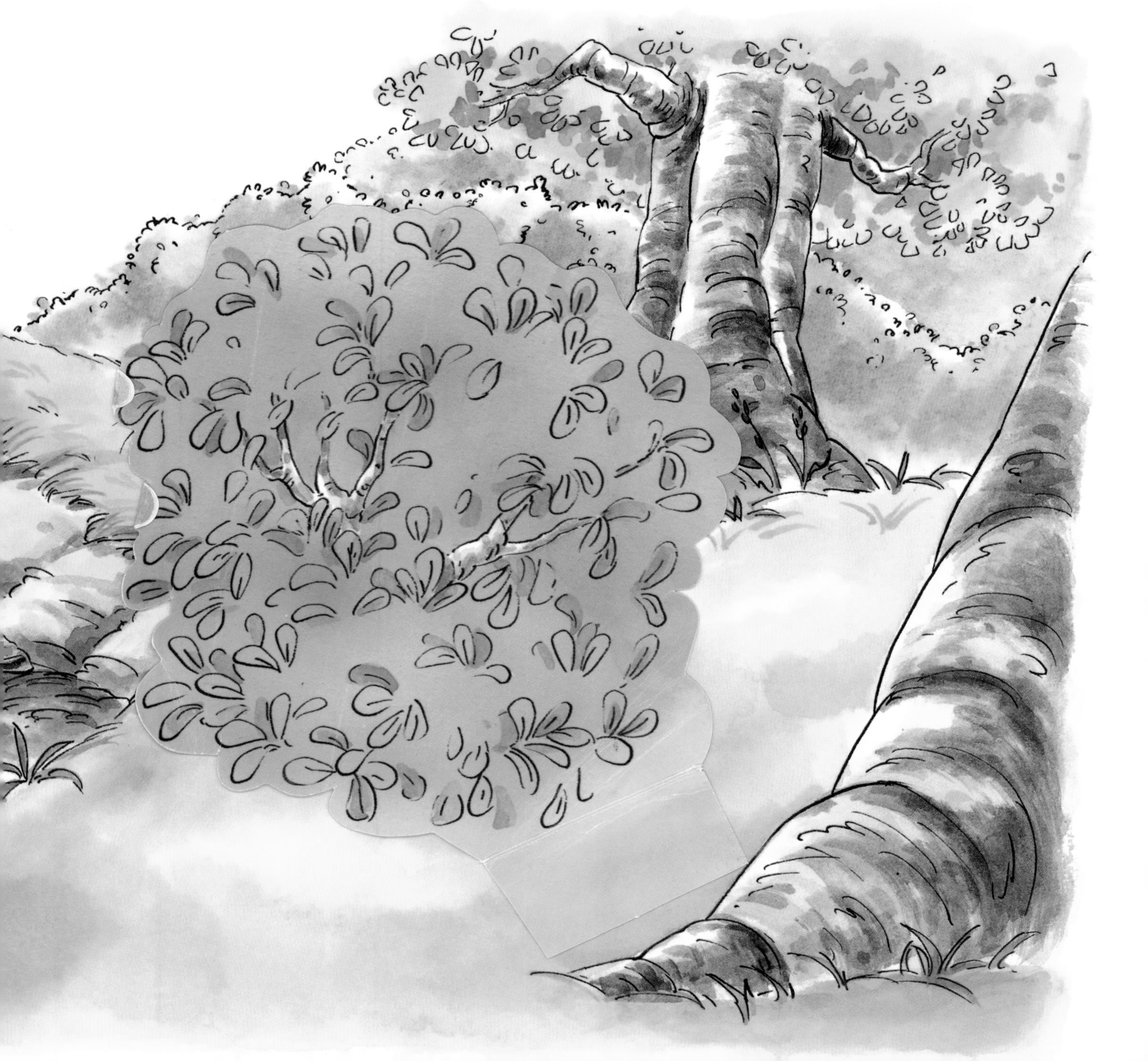

Where is Pooh?
Is he behind the gate?

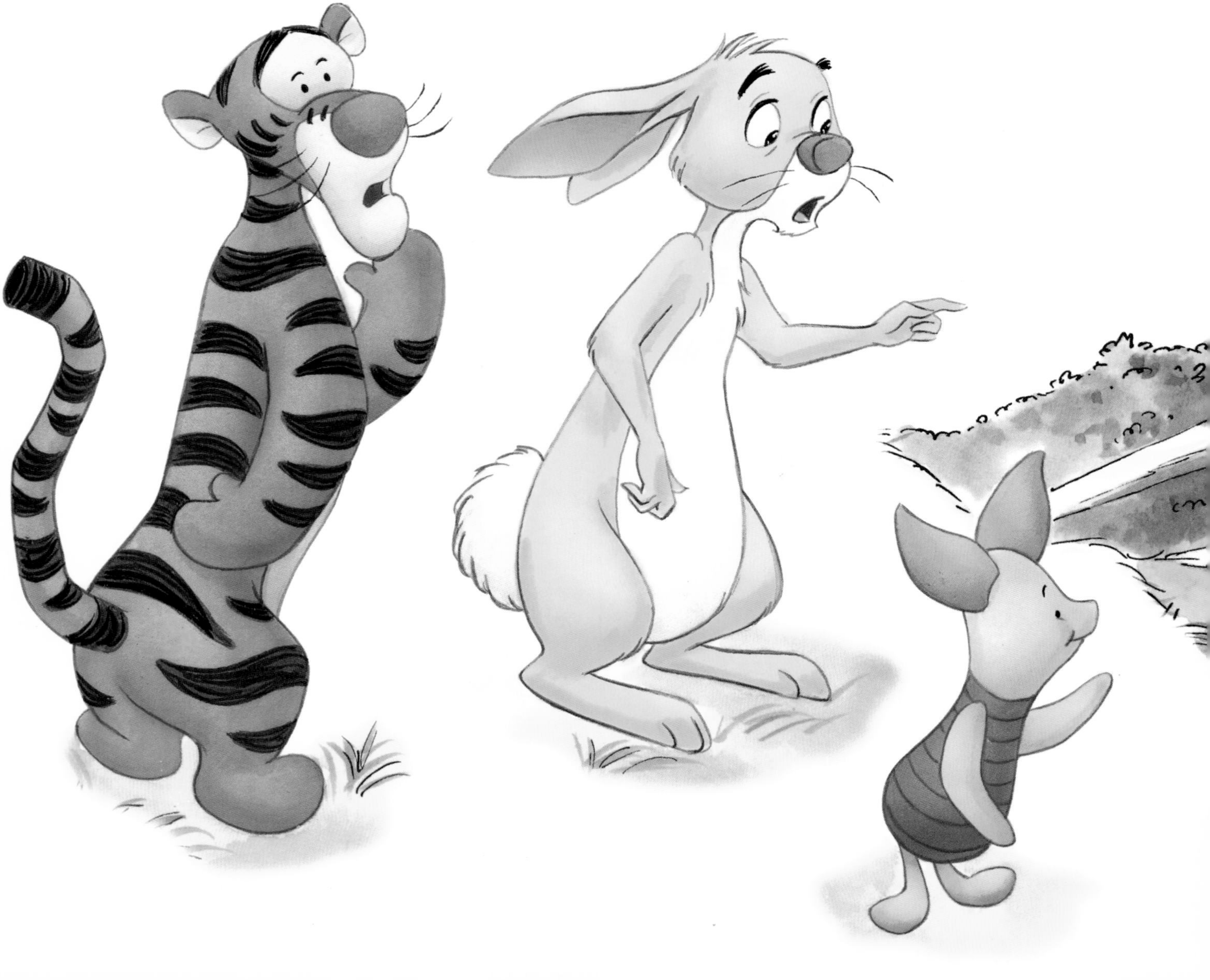

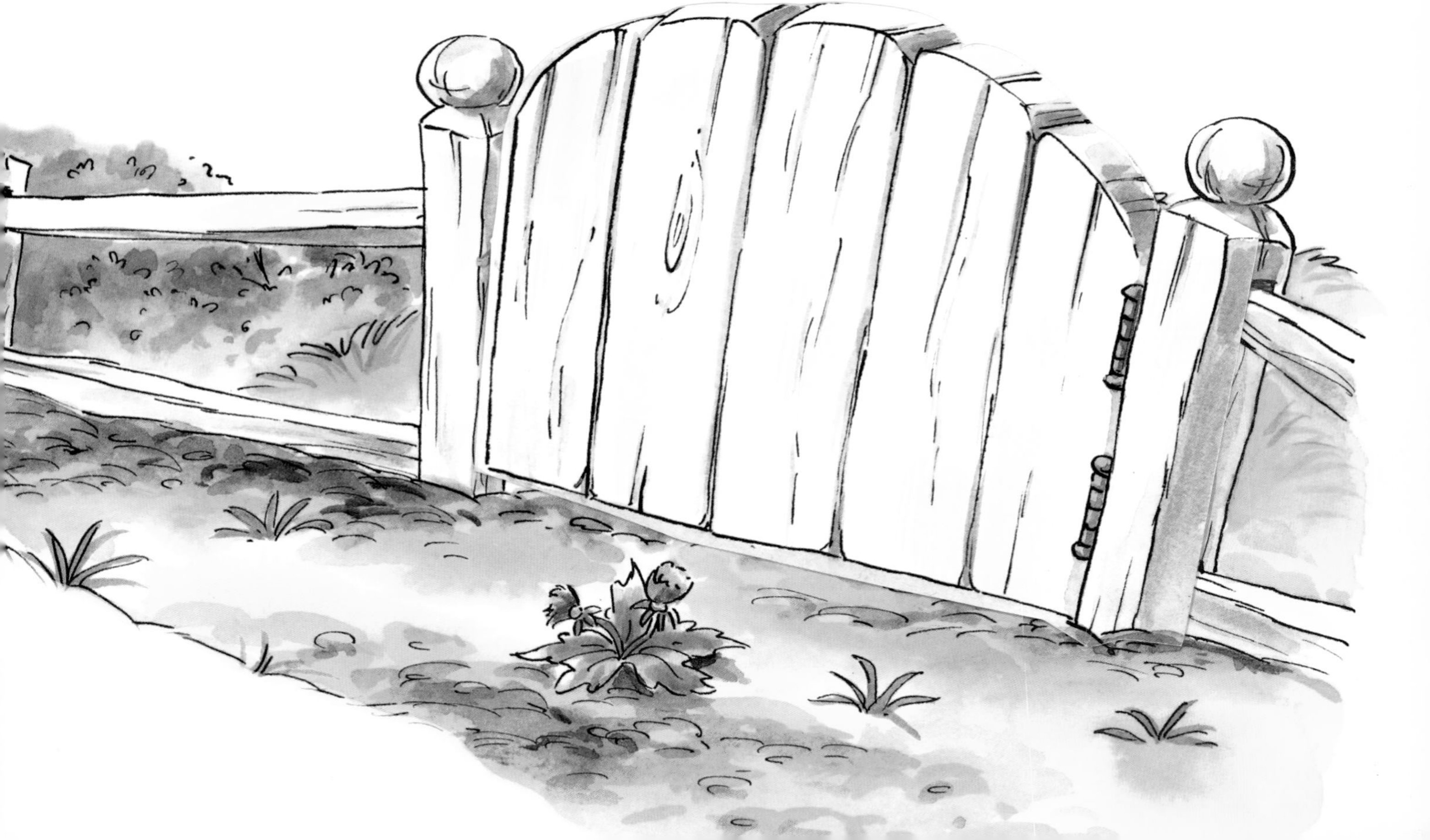

Where is Pooh?
Is he up in the tree?

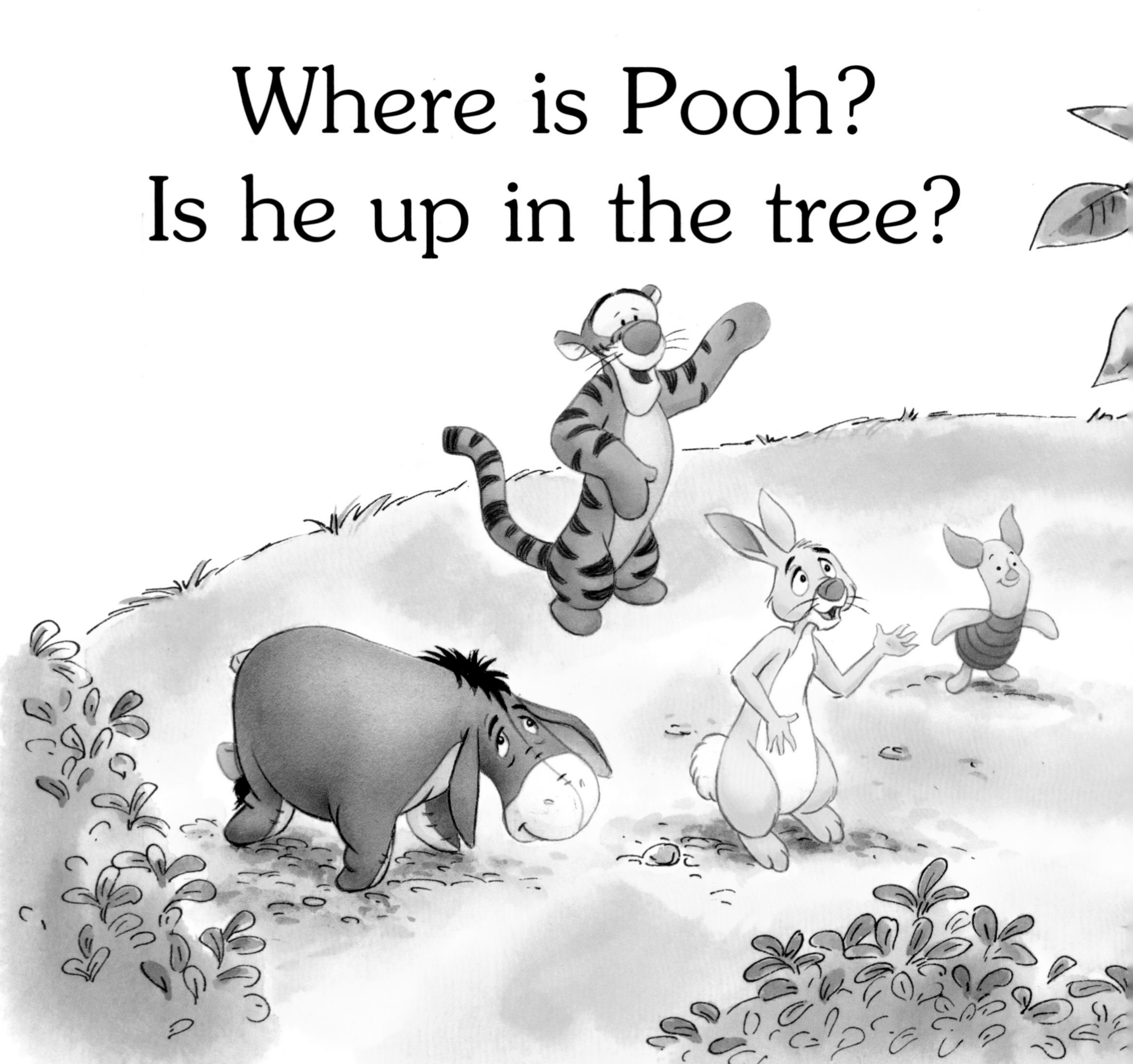

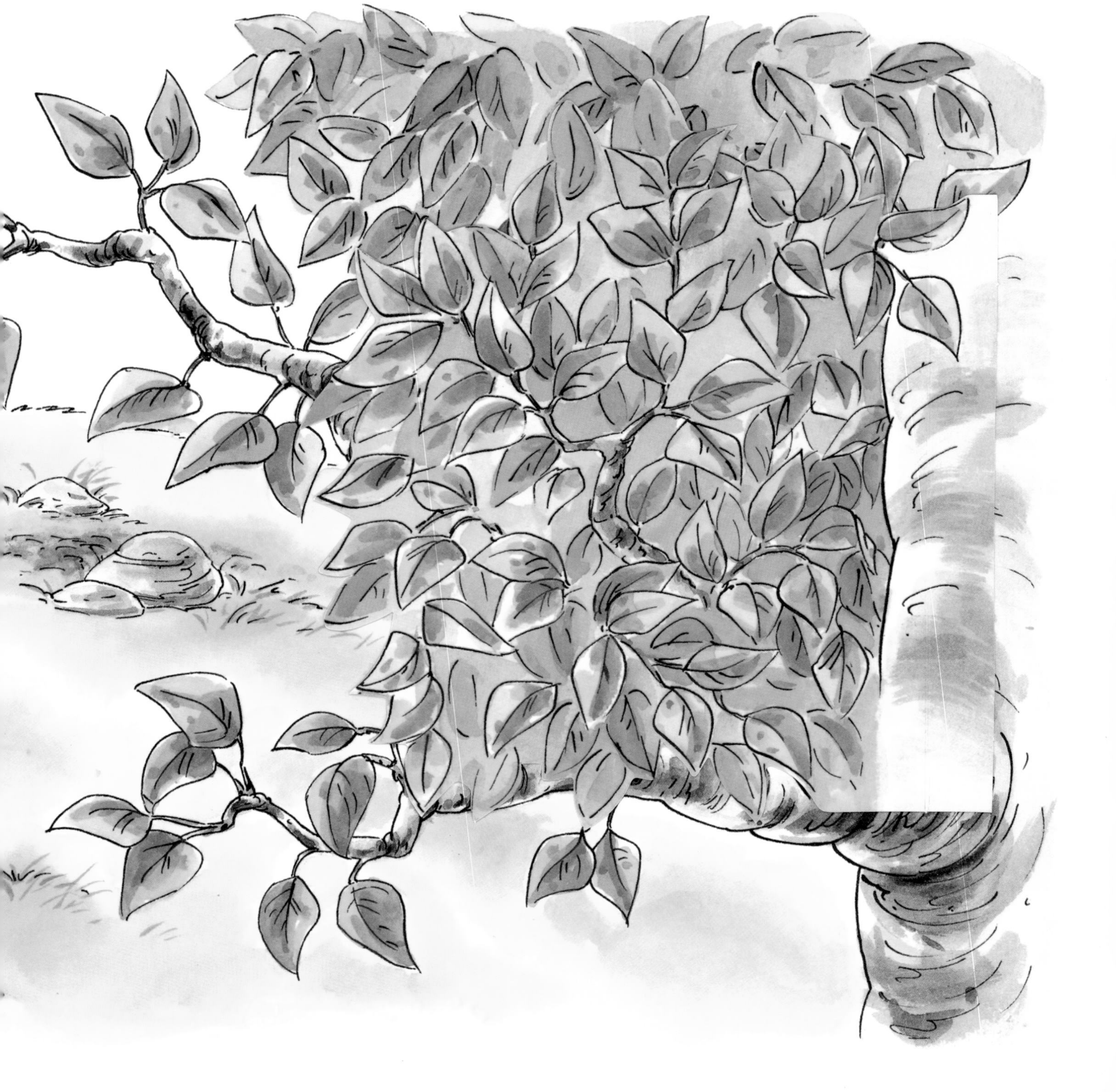

Where is Pooh?
Is he down in the hole?

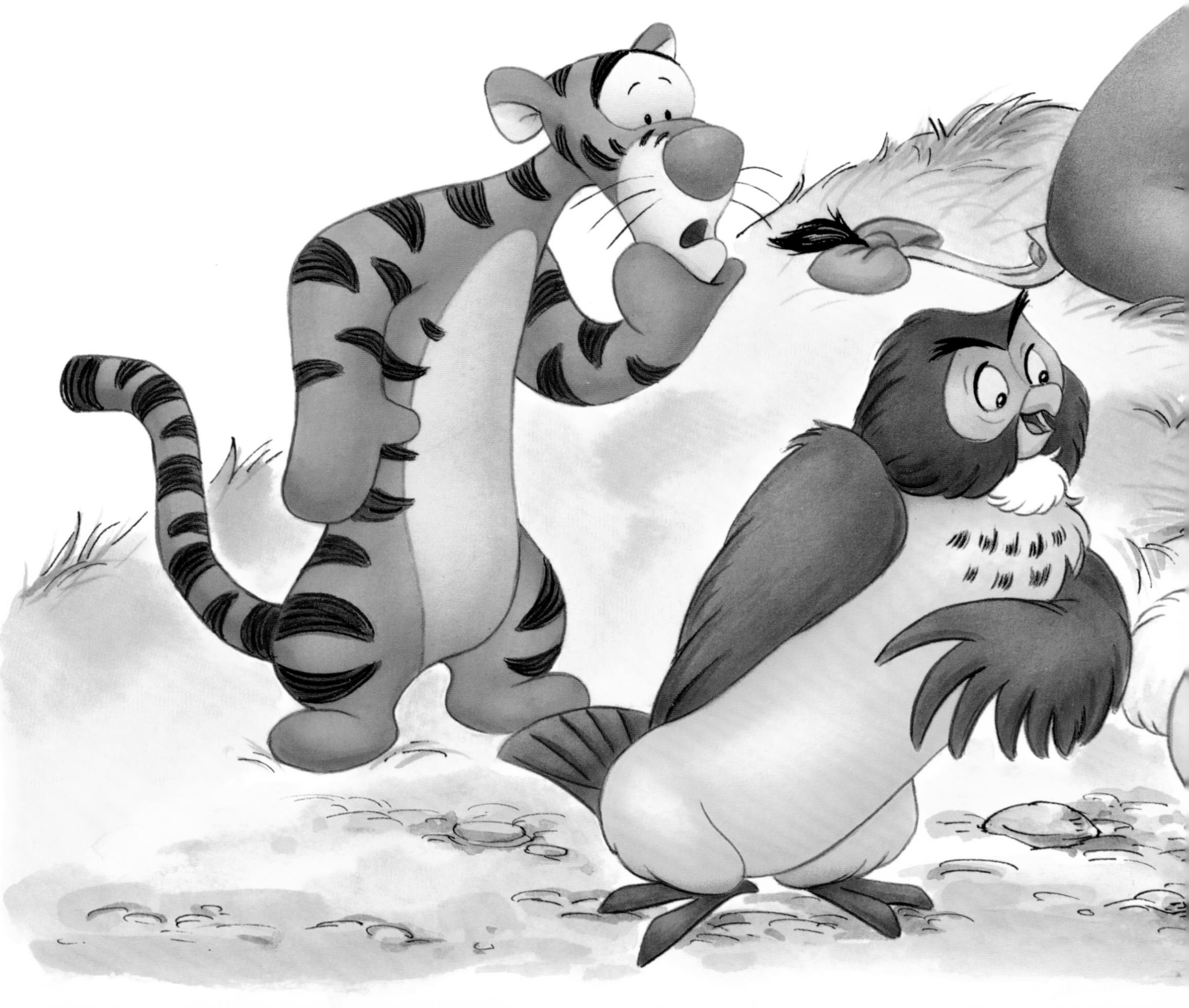

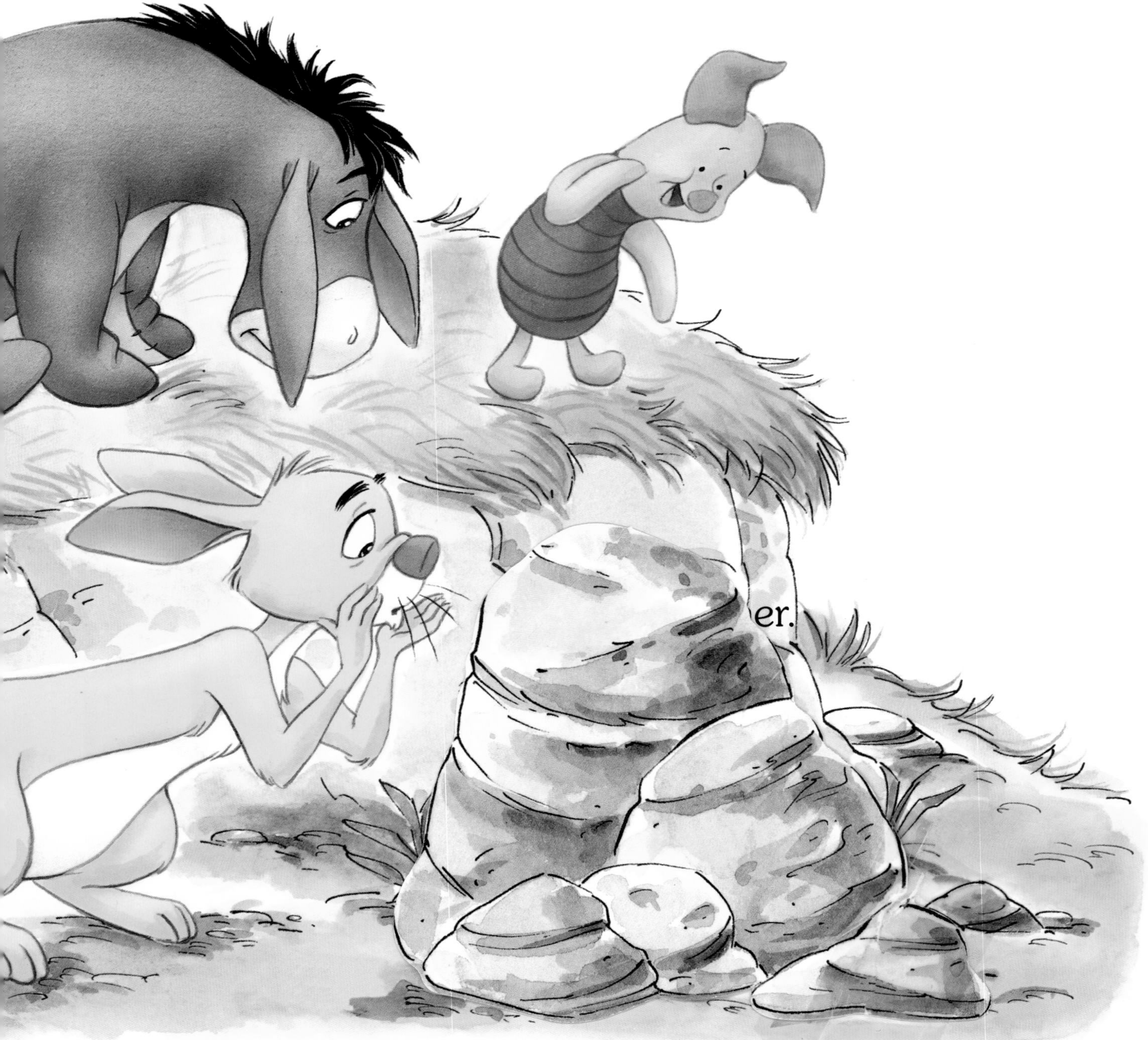

er.

Pooh! Where are you?

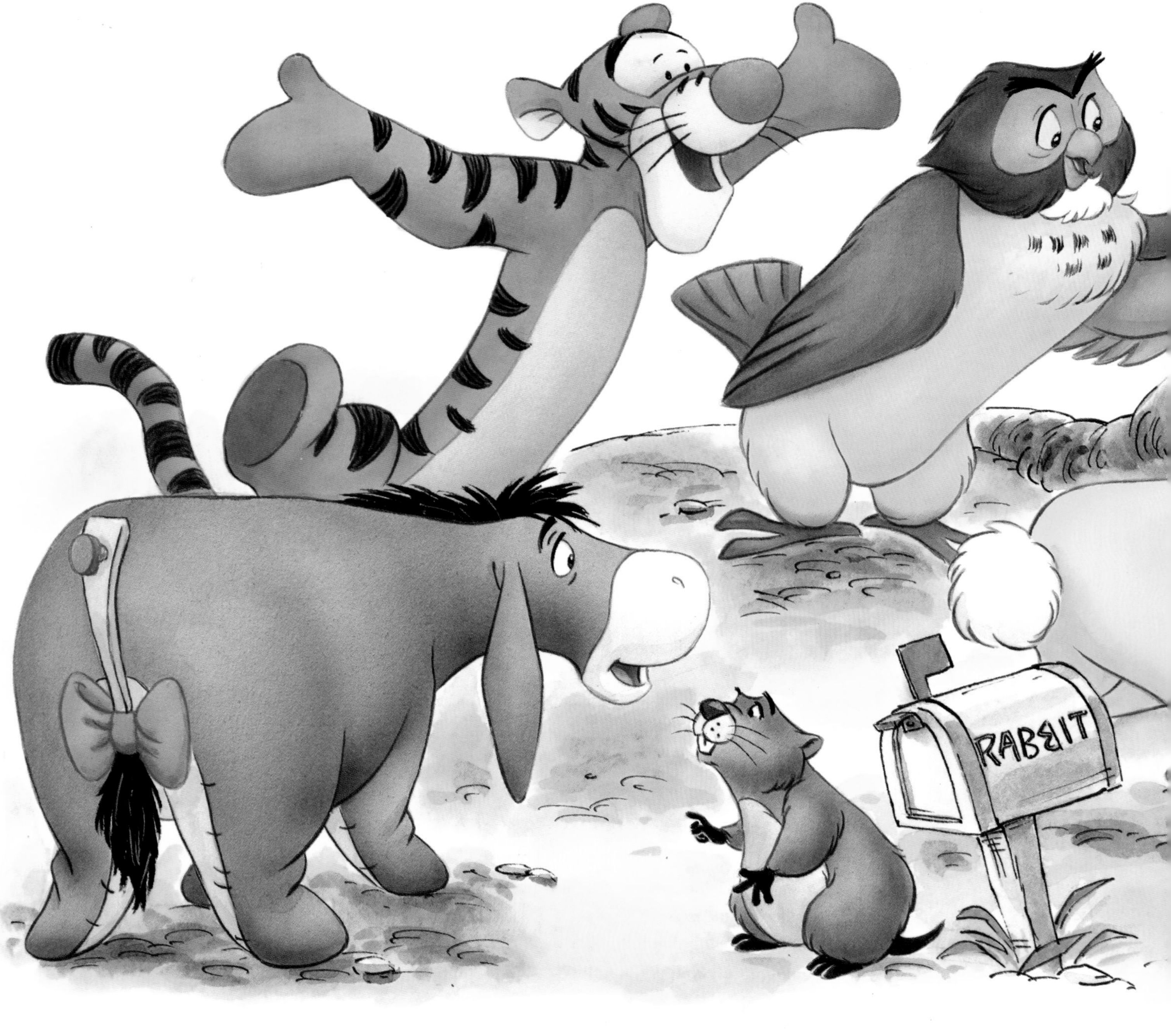

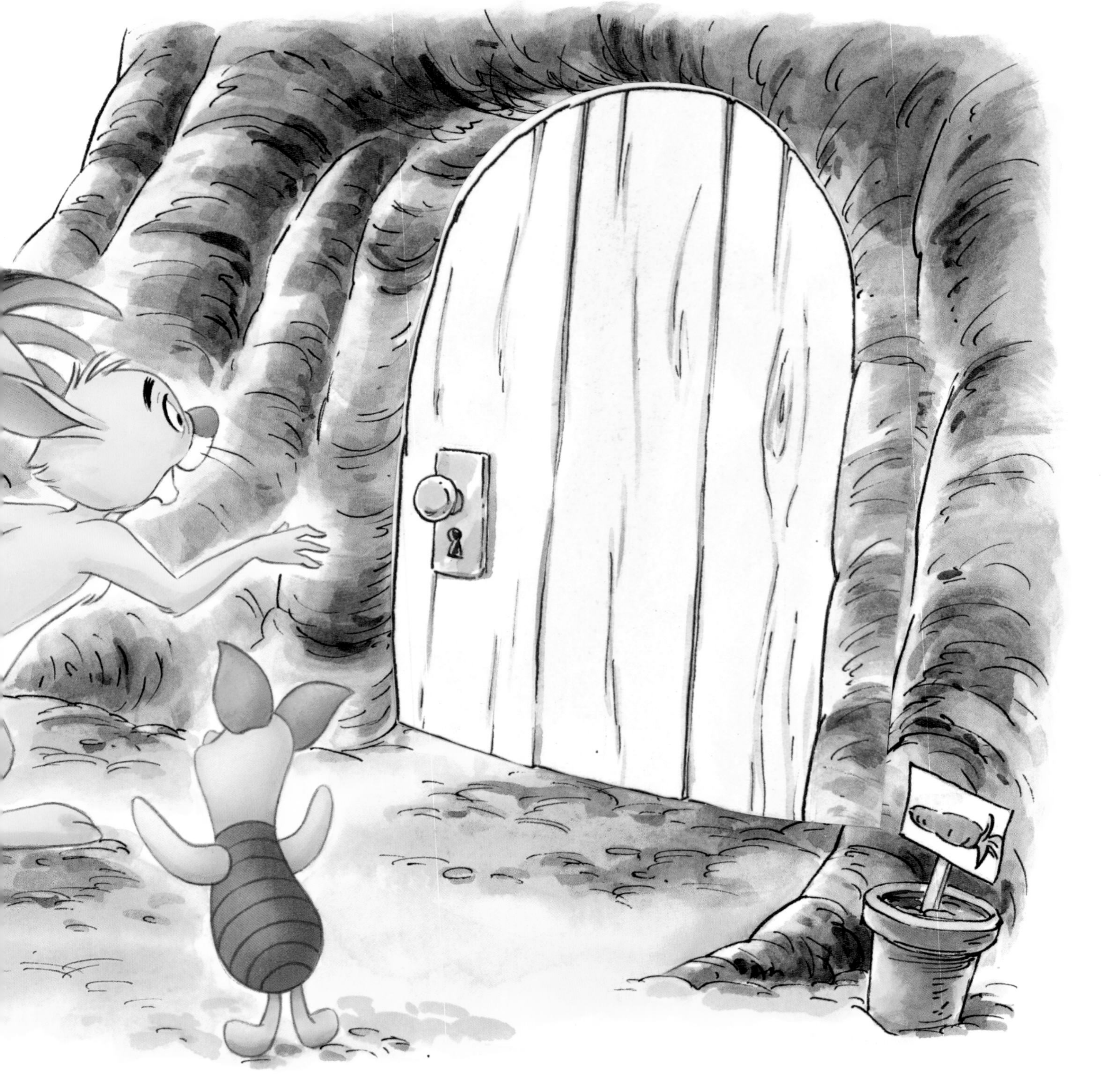

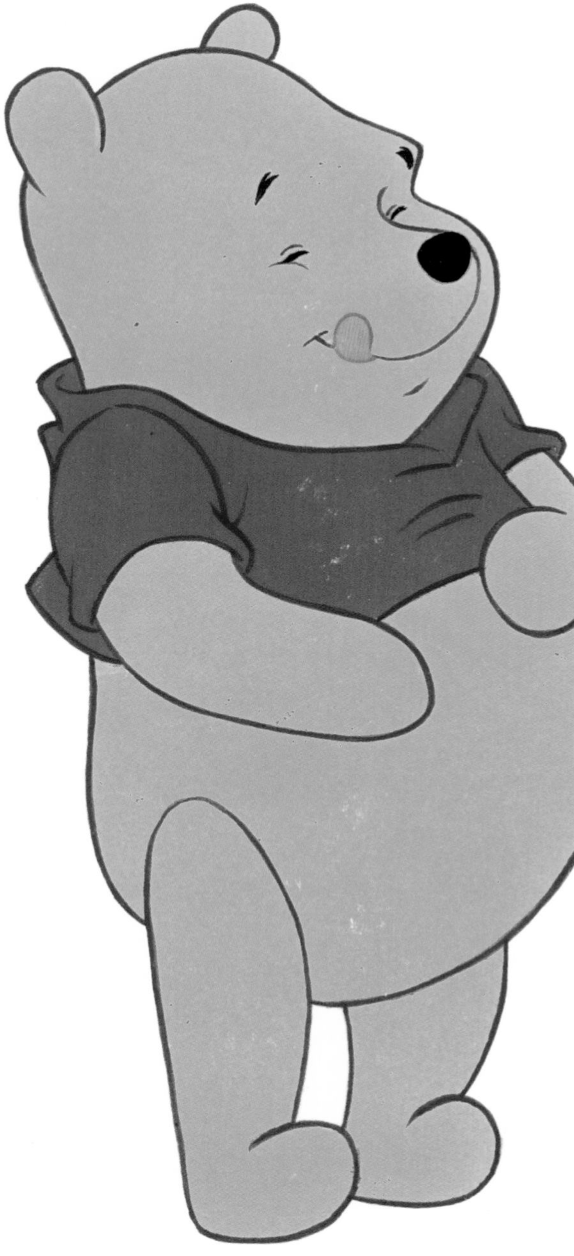

Yummy!